SAVE THE DAY!

the TINY GENIUSES

1. FLY TO THE RESCUE!

2. SET THE STAGE!

3. HIT A HOME RUN!

4. SAVE THE DAY!

READ ALL THE TINY GENIUSES BOOKS!

the TiNY GENiUSES

SAVE THE DAY!

by Megan E. Bryant

Scholastic Inc.

To Jackson and Deacon Hatch:
May books continue to open doors
and lead to new adventures.

If you purchased this book without a cover, you should be aware that this book is stolen property. It was reported as "unsold and destroyed" to the publisher, and neither the author nor the publisher has received any payment for this "stripped book."

Copyright © 2019 by Megan E. Bryant

All rights reserved. Published by Scholastic Inc., *Publishers since 1920.* SCHOLASTIC and associated logos are trademarks and/or registered trademarks of Scholastic Inc.

The publisher does not have any control over and does not assume any responsibility for author or third-party websites or their content.

No part of this publication may be reproduced, stored in a retrieval system, or transmitted in any form or by any means, electronic, mechanical, photocopying, recording, or otherwise, without written permission of the publisher. For information regarding permission, write to Scholastic Inc., Attention: Permissions Department, 557 Broadway, New York, NY 10012.

This book is a work of fiction. Names, characters, places, and incidents are either the product of the author's imagination or are used fictitiously, and any resemblance to actual persons, living or dead, business establishments, events, or locales is entirely coincidental.

ISBN 978-0-545-90967-9

10 9 8 7 6 5 4 3 2 1   19 20 21 22 23

Printed in the U.S.A.   40
First printing 2019

Book design by Maeve Norton

A clear and innocent conscience fears nothing.

—*Queen Elizabeth I*

You are never strong enough

that you don't need help.

—*Cesar Chavez*

CHAPTER 1

Jake Everdale shuffled forward in the lunch line and breathed in deeply, trying to use his nose to figure out what he'd be eating in a few minutes. He could've checked the menu posted on the wall, but where was the fun in that?

"Tacos?" he guessed.

"You wish," Jake's best friend, Emerson Lewis, said. "I think it's pizza."

As they approached the cashier, Jake resisted the urge to peek at the serving station. He wanted to pretend for as long as possible that tacos—or even pizza—were on the menu.

"Jake Everdale," Jake told the cashier.

"Oh—you're on the list," she replied. A mysterious smile crossed her face. "You're not having lunch in the cafeteria today."

"Huh?" Jake asked, confused.

She handed him a small packet with a picture of radishes on the front. Jake turned it over to find a note on the other side.

Greetings, Fourth Graders!

Please join me on Franklin Field for lunch today.

Sincerely yours,
Ms. Turner

Emerson shook his packet, which made a

rustling noise. "Seeds," he told Jake. "My mom just bought some for her garden."

"What are we supposed to do with seeds?" Jake asked.

Their school counselor, Mr. Pelman, was standing by the door. "Fourth graders! Right this way!" he called, spotting Jake and Emerson. "You'd better hurry up. Save me a slice?"

Jake and Emerson exchanged a hopeful glance. "A slice? Of pizza?" Emerson asked as they hurried outside.

"It *can't* be pizza. It's only Wednesday," Jake insisted.

He glanced longingly at the baseball diamond as the boys walked past it. Jake loved baseball more than just about anything in the world. But Jake had been benched ever since he'd broken the rules on a recent field trip—first because he'd sprained his ankle, and then as part of his punishment. At long last, Jake's ankle was finally healed, and his punishment was almost over.

It was just in time, too, because the biggest

game of the season was coming up. The Franklin Turkeys would be facing their longtime rivals, the Pinehurst Piranhas. Jake couldn't wait to get back on the field. He wanted to be in top shape when it was time to play the Piranhas—and hopefully bring back the trophy after it had spent two long years at Pinehurst Elementary. The trophy wasn't anything fancy—it was an old dog bowl that somebody had spray painted gold—but Jake knew in his heart that it belonged at Franklin Elementary.

Ms. Turner was waiting at the far end of Franklin Field, not far from the Wishing Well. Of course, *she* didn't know about the Wishing Well. To most people, it was just a rusty old storm drain. But students at Franklin Elementary School knew it was much more than that. According to legend, if you threw your most special belonging into the Wishing Well, it would grant any wish. Jake had only half believed the rumors until that fateful day when he'd tried it for himself. He was doing so poorly in school that Mom and Dad were about to make him quit baseball so he could focus on his grades. In a fit of desperation, Jake wished for better grades and threw his miniature Heroes of History action figures into the Wishing Well. He never expected them to come to life!

First, Amelia Earhart and Sir Isaac Newton inspired Jake's science project. Next, Ella Fitzgerald and Benjamin Franklin helped Jake tackle his history presentation. Then Frida Kahlo and Jackie Robinson coached Jake through his artist project. Jake never quite knew what to expect when he wished for extra help and met tiny versions of the world's greatest geniuses. But one thing was certain: They made life a lot more exciting—and unpredictable!

As Jake got closer, he realized Ms. Turner was standing next to a folding table stacked high with—were those *pizza boxes*?

"Yes!" Jake cheered, pumping his fist in the air. "You were right, dude. Looks like it's pizza day after all!"

"*And* it's from Mario's!" Emerson said. "That's even better than cafeteria pizza!"

"I hope there's pepperoni," Jake said as he peeked into one of the boxes.

"Pepperoni pizza is over there, Jake," Ms. Turner called, pointing to the far end of the table.

When Jake glanced in that direction, though, he suddenly lost his appetite. Aiden Allen, the meanest kid in fourth grade, was standing awfully close to the pepperoni pizza. Just seeing Aiden was enough to make Jake want to settle for plain cheese.

But Mario's pepperoni pizza *was* the best, so Jake—pointedly ignoring Aiden—approached the table.

Aiden glanced at Jake out of the corner of his eye. Then—it happened so fast that there was no way to stop it—he side-slammed the pizza box. It flew to the ground, and the last slice of pepperoni landed in the dirt.

"Whoops!" Aiden said loudly. "I am so sorry!"

Jake turned away stiffly to get a piece of cheese pizza instead. Of course, Aiden wasn't actually sorry. He never missed an opportunity to torment Jake.

After everyone had a plate of pizza, Ms. Turner started to speak. "I'm sure you're wondering why we're having this pizza party," she began.

"Because we're awesome?" Marco cracked.

"Well, sure, but that's not the only reason," Ms. Turner said, smiling. "We're also here to talk about our new social studies unit!"

Jake sighed. Of course there was a catch.

"I'm very excited about this unit, and I hope you will be, too," Ms. Turner continued. "It's something new for Franklin Elementary—something we've never done before. So we'll all be learning as we go. Or I should say, learning as we *grow*."

Ms. Turner had everyone's attention.

"I want you to take a look at that pizza you're eating," she said. "Where did it come from?"

"Mario's Pizzeria," Sam called out, pointing at the name on the boxes.

"Yes—but that's only part of the story," Ms. Turner said. "Who grew the grain to make the flour for the crust? Who planted the tomatoes and basil for the sauce—and who harvested them?

All I had to do was call Mario's and place an order, but the truth is that many, many other people were involved in making these pizzas possible. We're going to be learning a lot about farming and food production. Who grows our food? Who harvests it? How does it get from the farm to the grocery store to the dinner table?"

Jake glanced at Emerson out of the corner of his eye. He couldn't tell if this unit sounded especially interesting, or especially boring—but Ms. Turner was right about one thing: It was different from anything they'd done before. And it was nice to be sitting outside in the sunshine instead of cooped up in the cafeteria.

"But we won't just be reading about how food is grown," Ms. Turner continued. "We're going to try to do it ourselves."

She gestured to an area behind her, and that's when Jake noticed several square boxes. Each wooden box measured three feet long and three feet wide.

"Raised beds!" Emerson exclaimed.

Ms. Turner's face lit up. "That's right!" she said. "Emerson, tell us more."

"My mom got some for Mother's Day last year," he replied. "They make it easy to start a garden."

"Very good," Ms. Turner said. "That's exactly what we'll be doing—starting the very first Franklin Elementary Vegetable Garden. As we learn how food is produced, we'll try to grow some, too. We'll learn science about plants and keep garden journals where we'll write down our predictions and observations."

"Are we gonna *eat* the vegetables?" Hannah asked, looking worried. One of the boys pretended to puke on his pizza, making everyone crack up.

"Great question," Ms. Turner said over the commotion. "We can sample some of the veggies when we celebrate our first harvest with a big picnic. But most of the food we grow will be donated to hungry families."

Silence fell over the kids.

"There are forty million people in the country who don't have enough food to eat," Ms. Turner explained. "Some of them live in our community. Some of them are students at our school. There are a lot of reasons why so many families struggle with hunger, and there isn't just one solution to a problem this big. But the good news is that we can help—and we can get started right now! When you finish eating, grab a partner and claim a garden bed. Clara and Gabriel, would you please pass out the assignment?"

There was a sudden scramble as everyone abandoned their pizza to find a partner. Jake was extra-glad that he was sitting next to Emerson, who wasn't just his best friend but one of the best students in the entire fourth grade. Most of the time, Jake felt that his assignments for school were pretty pointless—not exactly a waste of time, but close.

But this one?

This one mattered.

CHApTER 2

After school, Jake and Emerson hurried to change into their practice gear. As Jake pulled on his old baseball pants, he tried to shrug off that familiar twinge of embarrassment. He felt so dumb suiting up just to sit and watch, but at least today was the last day of his punishment.

Jake plunked down on the bench and stared out at the diamond. Zoe and Gabriel were warming up, tossing the ball back and forth between first and second base. Coach Carlson was standing on the pitcher's mound, talking intently to—

Wait a second. Who *was* that?

Jake squinted, frowning as he tried to figure out which one of his teammates was chatting with Coach. Then the player turned a little, gesturing to home plate—

"Oh no." Jake groaned.

"What's the matter?" Emerson asked.

Jake was already running over to the team captain, a fifth grader named Liam Hatcher.

"Hatch!" Jake called urgently. "Who's—who's on the mound? With Coach?"

Hatch glanced over casually. "Oh. New player. Aiden something. Coach saw him hanging around practice and asked if he wanted to play for the Turkeys."

Just like that, Jake's worst fears were confirmed.

Aiden Allen had joined the team.

Are you kidding? Jake wanted to yell. How was it possible that Coach had noticed Aiden but completely missed how mean he was to Jake? The *only* reason Aiden stuck around after school was to make fun of Jake for being benched. And now he got to be on the team for it?

By the time Jake got back to the bench, Emerson had figured out what was going on. "Don't worry," he said. "Aiden's on *your* turf now. How many years have you been playing baseball? Since, like, before you could walk?"

"Pretty much," Jake answered.

"You're going to own the field," Emerson said. "Just like always. I mean, who *cares* if Aiden's on the team now?"

"I care," Jake said. "Baseball has always been an Aiden-free zone. And now he's going to be right here, at every practice, at every game, just waiting for me to mess up so he can make fun of me in front of the whole team."

"Whoa, I'm gonna stop you right there," Emerson said. "First of all, you don't mess up in baseball. You're a baseball hero."

"Couldn't agree more!" Aiden's voice rang out. "Jake *is* a zero!"

x

Jake stared straight ahead, willing himself to ignore Aiden. But it was hard to stay cool on the outside when his temper was boiling on the inside. Jake could feel his ears burning, and his jaw ached as he clenched his teeth—signs that Aiden was sure to notice.

Emerson looked at Jake. "Not worth it," he mouthed. Then he turned back to Aiden. "Maybe you should get your hearing checked," Emerson said evenly. "Because I said Jake was a hero. Not a zero."

Aiden just threw back his head and laughed. "If that's what you think, you should get your brain checked," he retorted.

Maybe Jake would have felt less hopeless if he'd been able to play at practice; focusing all his attention on the game would've kept his mind busy. But warming the bench yet again gave him plenty of opportunities to worry about Aiden joining the team. It didn't help that Aiden kept glancing over at Jake, smirking. It was clear he knew how much his presence would upset Jake.

As Jake and Emerson walked home from practice, Emerson kept up a steady stream of chatter. If he noticed how quiet Jake was, he didn't let on.

"Do you want to hang out before dinner?" Emerson asked as they approached his house. "We could get started on our farm project."

Jake didn't really feel like working on anything for school. "Um . . . I have to ask my mom," he said. "I'll call you if she says I can."

"Great!" Emerson replied. "Just tell her that it's for homework and she'll definitely say yes! See ya."

"See ya," Jake replied as Emerson walked away. Then he continued home alone. He found Mom in the living room, talking on her cell.

"Mom, can I—" he began.

Mom frowned, pointed at her phone, and mouthed, "Homework!"

Jake was too bummed to even pet his dog, Flapjack. Instead, he trudged up to his room and threw his backpack on the desk. The broken zipper popped open, scattering his school papers everywhere. The farm project assignment was right on top.

Part 1: Plan Your Garden

Learn the gardening zone for our area and conduct research on which plants grow best here. Prepare a list of 4-6 crops you'd like to grow in your garden bed. How much space do they need to grow? What do they need to thrive? Which problems could your plants face? Write at least three sentences about each type of crop, including one about why you chose it for the food pantry garden.

Jake groaned. This was only Part 1, and it was a *ton* of work! Maybe he should go see if Mom was off the phone. It would definitely be better to tackle it with Emerson.

Just then, Jake's door opened with a loud *bang*. It was his little sister, Julia.

"I *thought* I heard you come home!" she cried triumphantly. "Mom has been on the phone *forever*! It's been the boringest day of all time! Let's play with my Funny Bunnies!"

For once, Jake was glad to have homework as an excuse to say no. Julia's collection of small, rainbow-colored Funny Bunnies was her latest obsession—but to Jake, they were the dullest toy ever invented.

"Sorry, I can't," Jake said, turning back to his desk. "I have a huge new project and it's going to take up all my time. And trust me, it's *way* more boring than you can even imagine."

"What is it?" Julia asked.

Jake sighed. "I have to plan a garden or something," he said. "So . . . if you could, like, get out, please . . ."

A strange silence followed. After a few moments, Jake turned around to see what Julia was doing.

But to his surprise, she had disappeared.

That's weird, Jake thought. When Julia was bored, she usually had to be dragged out of his room kicking and screaming.

Jake turned back to his assignment and got out a fresh piece of paper. When Mom was off the phone, he'd ask her what zone they lived in—whatever that meant.

He was so preoccupied that he didn't notice a suspicious clanking sound on the stairs.

"I'm *here* to *help!*" Julia's voice rang out cheerfully.

"Seriously, I'm *working*," he said through clenched teeth. "Go away!"

Clang-clink-thunk-thwak-splat!

Jake leaped backwards as Julia dumped a canvas bag full of gardening tools on his desk. They weren't just tools, though—there were also clumps of dirt, gritty pebbles, soggy peat moss, and a half-full watering can that was pouring water on everything—

"Julia!" Jake bellowed. "What are you *doing*?"

"Helping!" Julia said proudly. "You can't garden without the right tools. That's what Mom always says!"

The blood rushed into Jake's face as his temper rose. "This is *no* help! None!" he yelled. "You've made a huge mess, and—is that a *worm*?"

Julia's lower lip jutted out. "You always complain about your homework," she said. "But gardening is fun. I help Mom a lot. I know more than you think I do."

Jake was so busy mopping up the puddle with an old sweat sock that he didn't notice how close she was to tears. "Look, I don't want to be rude, but you're in *kindergarten*," he said. "Fourth grade is a *lot* harder than you can even imagine."

"So why don't you make a wish?" Julia asked.

Jake paused and looked at her. The way she said it—like it would solve all his problems. Like it would be so easy. Well, it would be easy. All he had to do was say the words, and a miniature toy version of one of history's greatest geniuses would appear.

I'll probably fail if I don't make a wish, Jake thought. *Getting extra help isn't against the rules. It might even help Emerson and me grow lots of food. And that would help even more hungry people.*

Jake took a deep breath. "I wish for extra help," he said.

Too late, he realized that he wasn't the only one saying those words.

POP!

POP!

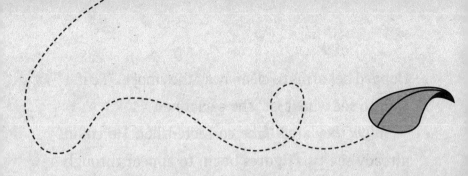

CHAPTER 3

Hundreds of sparks twinkled on Jake's desk, bright enough to be seen through the thick smoke. Jake grabbed his sister's arm. "Julia!" he gasped. "What have you done?"

"I made a wish, too!" she said.

"That's not how this is supposed to work!" Jake cried. "Oh, this is going to be bad!"

Julia, however, didn't seem concerned. She

flapped her arms to clear away the smoke. "I can't wait to see who it is!" she exclaimed

"Who *they* are," Jake corrected her. He could already see two figures begin to appear through the fading smoke. Even though he was worried, Jake's excitement grew as he wondered which geniuses from history he was about to meet. The sparks were still gleaming when one of them came into view. Despite her tiny size, she somehow seemed larger than life. Maybe it was the vibrant red curls piled on top of her head, or the stiff lace collar that framed her face like a fan, or the billowing skirts of her fancy gown. But there was one thing that Jake couldn't stop staring at: her glittering gold crown.

"A queen," Julia whispered. "I've always wanted to meet a real queen!"

Jake cleared his throat. "Hi," he began. "My name is Jake, and—"

If the queen was startled to see a giant boy and his giant sister standing before her, she didn't show it. She pulled herself up to her full height—almost four whole inches if you counted the crown—and held her head regally. "How d—" she began.

"How did you get here?" Jake guessed. "I don't really know, but I'll try to explain. A couple of months ago—"

"*Silence!*"

The queen's voice wasn't especially loud, but there was a tone to it that made Jake's mouth go dry and his legs go wobbly.

"How *dare* you speak to us before being spoken to?" the monarch continued in that same commanding tone. "How *dare* you display such utter contempt for royal protocol?"

Julia's foot collided with Jake's ankle. "Bow!" she muttered as she dropped into a floor-sweeping curtsy. Her forehead nearly touched the ground.

Of course! Jake thought as he bent as low as he could. He took advantage of the opportunity to rummage through the stuff under his desk until he found the pamphlet that had come with his Heroes of History action figures. It contained a short biography of every single figure in the set. Of course, Jake could have just asked the queen who she was—but he had a feeling that question would make her even angrier.

Jake recognized her stately image at once.

> Queen Elizabeth I
> 1533–1603, England
> One of the most powerful and beloved
> rulers of England, Queen Elizabeth was
> known as Gloriana, or the "glorious queen."

"You may rise," the queen's voice echoed from above.

Jake scrambled to his feet and tried to think of all the fanciest, floweriest words he knew. "My most sincere apologies, Your Highness," he said. "My sister and I were—we, uh, we were so, uh . . ."

"Dazzled!" Julia piped up.

"Yeah! Dazzled! To be in your, um, most

majestic and, uh, *glorious* presence," Jake said. "We forgot the royal protocols."

Jake held his breath, waiting for Queen Elizabeth to respond. Would she accept his apology?

"You are not the first to lose your composure before us," she said with a haughty sniff. "Mind that it never happens again."

"Yes, Your Highness," Julia promised.

"Julia," Jake said under his breath. "Who is this 'us' she keeps talking about?"

"I think she's using the royal 'we'!" Julia said. "Kings and queens were so powerful that they thought they could speak for God! So they used 'we' and 'us' instead of 'I' and 'me.'"

"How do you even know that?" Jake asked.

"*The Royal Book of Royals*, of course," Julia said. "I know practically *everything* about royalty."

Jake tried to smile, but inside, he wasn't nearly as confident as his sister. Even if Julia knew about royal protocols, or all the special rules and manners for interacting with royalty, Jake was totally clueless.

I don't see how Queen Elizabeth can help with the farm project, Jake decided. *She's only here because of Julia's wish. That makes her Julia's problem— not mine.*

Jake turned his attention to the other tiny genius on his desk, a man who was wearing a plaid shirt, blue jeans, and heavy boots. His thick, black hair was streaked with silver, and his whole face seemed to crinkle when he smiled up at Jake.

"Hi," Jake said. "I'm Jake. It's, uh, nice to meet you."

"*Hola*, Jake," the man replied. "My name is Cesar Chavez."

Jake had the feeling he should've known who Cesar Chavez was, but he couldn't quite remember. He ducked under the desk again to look in the pamphlet.

> *Cesar Chavez*
> *1927–1993, United States*
> *This Hero of History was an organizer who proved that great change is possible when people stand together.*

Jake had barely finished reading when he heard a shout. He scrambled to get up and—

Thwak!

"Ow!" Jake yelped as he hit his head on the desk. Queen Elizabeth, however, didn't even notice.

"*Where* is our Privy Council?" she demanded. "Our chief minister? Our spymaster? Our lady-in-waiting?"

Jake and Julia exchanged a panicked glance. They'd tried their best to make the other geniuses feel at home—from a little laboratory for Sir Isaac Newton to a pint-sized paint set for Frida Kahlo—but they weren't prepared to provide Queen Elizabeth with a full royal court.

"This palace is certainly . . . palatial," the queen continued, staring up at Jake's bedroom ceiling. Jake looked up, too, and realized that the ordinary ceiling must seem enormously high to someone who was just a few inches tall.

"But the conditions!" Queen Elizabeth continued, making a face of disgust as she surveyed the mess in Jake's room. "You are clearly in no way prepared to host nobility such as ourselves."

"No . . . I guess not," Jake said, using his foot to nudge an especially stinky sock under his bed. "It's just, you see, we weren't really expecting you—"

Queen Elizabeth narrowed her eyes. "Nonsense," she scoffed. "Arrangements were surely made months ago—unless—we are in hiding—"

"In hiding?" Jake repeated in confusion. But Queen Elizabeth misunderstood his tone for confirmation.

"Our enemies are plotting against us again, I see," she said with a curt nod. "Given the circumstances, we will attempt to overlook these slovenly conditions. Now, *where* is our lady-in-waiting?"

"She was . . . unable to accompany Your Highness," Jake said as inspiration struck. "But allow me to present the Lady Julia."

"Me?" Julia squeaked with excitement. She

dropped into another curtsy. "Your Highness, I am at your service!"

Queen Elizabeth sized her up with a frown. "Your manners are atrocious and your dress is a disgrace," she finally said. "But under our tutelage, you may become passable yet. We should like to retire to the royal chambers now."

"Yes, Your Highness," Julia said. Then she shot a starstruck smile at Jake and whispered, "She thinks I could be *passable*!"

While Julia brought Queen Elizabeth to the dollhouse, Jake turned his attention back to Mr. Chavez. "Sorry about that," he said. "I didn't realize that queens could be so demanding."

"Sometimes powerful people forget that they are people—just like the rest of us," Mr. Chavez said with a knowing look.

"Did you learn that when you were, uh, organizing?" Jake asked.

Mr. Chavez nodded. "And even before," he said.

"I wish I could be organized," Jake told him. "My room is such a big mess that I stopped trying."

"No, no, Jake," Mr. Chavez told him, smiling again. "I organize *people*. Not things." He chuckled at the look of confusion on Jake's face. "When I saw how hard the workers toiled on the farms, under terrible conditions, I knew something had to change. It was my honor to help them stand up for their rights."

"The farms?" Jake repeated. "So—you know about farming? And growing food?"

"I sure do," Mr. Chavez replied. "Working the land is how I got my start—and how I found my purpose."

Jake grinned in response. Just like that, the farm project seemed a lot more manageable!

CHAPTER 4

The next day, Jake was halfway through his math quiz when a strange sound caught his attention.

Beep! Beep! Beep! Beep!

A dump truck was backing up onto Franklin Field!

Jake wasn't the only one who forgot all about math. Every student started whispering as the truck inched across the grass.

Ms. Turner crossed the room and closed the blinds. "I'm excited about our social studies lesson, too," she told them. "But right now, we're focusing on math."

Jake dragged his attention back to the math problems. He could still hear the truck, but Jake knew he had to focus on the quiz. He couldn't risk getting a bad grade. Not when the big game against the Pinehurst Piranhas was just a couple of weeks away.

"Five more minutes," Ms. Turner called out.

Jake finished the last problem and even had a few extra minutes to check over his work. He didn't want to get his hopes too high, but he was pretty sure he had passed.

"Good news, everyone," Ms. Turner announced after she collected the quizzes. She opened the blinds with a loud *snnnap*! "As you may have noticed, a large dump truck has just left an enormous mound of dirt on Franklin Field. You know what that means, right?"

Aiden's hand shot into the air. "Someone has to move it into our garden beds," he announced. "We have baseball practice after school."

"That's right," Ms. Turner said. "I can't imagine Coach Carlson would appreciate all that extra dirt on the field, especially with the big game approaching! Someone *does* have to move it . . . and that someone is all of you."

Some kids laughed; some kids groaned; but when Ms. Turner held up a shovel, they all realized she was serious.

"A big part of farming is manual labor—or, in other words, really hard work," she explained. "That's why we'll have extra time in the garden today for our social studies lesson. Our goal is to get all that dirt moved into the garden beds, or else we'll be hearing about it from Coach Carlson tomorrow."

"She's not kidding," Emerson whispered to Jake, who grinned in response. A double period in the fresh air and sunshine, instead of staring at the SMART Board, sounded pretty great to Jake—even if they had to spend it shoveling dirt.

At first, all the kids were laughing and messing around as shovelfuls of dirt flew through the air. But it wasn't long before Jake realized he had seriously underestimated just how hard it would be. The first few shovels of dirt were easy to move, but they barely made a dent in the big pile.

"There's still so much dirt to move," Emerson muttered to Jake. "Coach is *not* going to be happy about this."

Jake wiped the sweat off his forehead, leaving a streak of dirt on his face. "We'll just have to move faster," he said.

But the muscles in his arms and back were already starting to ache, and Jake was pretty sure he was getting a blister on his thumb. He felt more than relieved when Ms. Turner blew her whistle to announce it was time for a water break.

"This is impossible," Emerson groaned as he dropped his shovel.

Jake flopped onto the ground. "All we've done is move dirt, and I'm exhausted," he said.

Emerson joined him. "Everything about this project is harder than I thought it would be," he said.

"Yeah," Jake agreed. "And we've barely even gotten started. But . . ."

"What?" Emerson asked as Jake's voice trailed off.

Jake glanced around to make sure that no one could hear them. "Let's just say that wishes have been made . . . and granted," he said mysteriously. The average person wouldn't have understood what Jake was trying to say, but Emerson figured it out right away.

"For real?" he asked, forgetting to be quiet. "A farming expert?"

Jake put a finger to his lips and nodded his head.

"Sorry," Emerson whispered. "Who is he? Or she?"

"They," Jake corrected him.

Emerson's eyes got even wider. *"They?"* he repeated. "Two? At once?"

Jake nodded.

"Dude! What are you waiting for?" Emerson exclaimed. "Bring 'em on!"

Jake shot him a look. "Have you lost your mind?" he asked. "I am *not* going to bring them to school. Every time the geniuses go anywhere, it turns into an epic disaster."

"But what about bringing them after practice?" Emerson asked hopefully. "You know, after everybody else has gone home?"

Ms. Turner blew her whistle again. "Back to work, everybody!" she announced.

Jake looked at the shovel, the fresh blister on his thumb, and the massive mound of dirt. "Sure," he told Emerson.

After practice, Jake raced home to ask Mr. Chavez for advice about the farm project. Julia was in his room, but Jake—knowing she was keeping an eye on Queen Elizabeth—didn't mind.

"Thank goodness you're back," Julia said. "I'm really—"

"Tell me later," Jake said, brushing past her. "I've got to get back to Franklin Field. Emerson's waiting for me."

Jake knelt down beside Mr. Chavez and explained the project.

"I'd be happy to help," Mr. Chavez said. "It's been a while since I worked in the fields, and I did more harvesting than planting, but I'll give you any advice I can."

"Great," Jake said. "Let's go."

"Wait," Queen Elizabeth spoke up.

"Wow, nice scepter," Jake said, admiring the glittering staff that Queen Elizabeth carried. On closer inspection, it turned out to be a cotton swab coated in glitter and sequins. He turned to Julia. "Did you make that?"

Julia nodded miserably. "The queen hates it, though," she said. "I don't know why she's carrying it. Maybe she's trying to find a trash can to put it in."

"We should like to accompany you," Queen Elizabeth announced.

Oh no, Jake thought. He glanced at Julia just in time to catch a look of panic on her face.

"Jake! This is a terrible idea!" Julia whispered urgently.

"Say no more," Jake assured her.

Then he turned to the queen.

"Your Majesty," he began. "Trust me, you do *not* want to go to the garden. It's *very* dirty and *full* of bugs—"

"It's no place for a queen!" Julia added.

"Farming isn't just dirt and bugs. It's dignified work—noble, even," Mr. Chavez spoke up. His voice was kind, but firm. "What could be higher service than feeding the hungry?"

Uh-oh, Jake thought. Mr. Chavez was right to call them out.

"We didn't mean—" Jake began. But the queen didn't let him finish.

"To *wear* the crown is to *be* the Crown," Queen Elizabeth declared. "There is nothing higher than that. We are the head of the Church of England! We have been anointed by God himself!"

"Your Majesty," Julia spoke up, "wouldn't you like to stay here, in your chambers?"

"For your own safety!" Jake added.

Queen Elizabeth banged her scepter on the desk, making a pair of sequins fall off. "We will not be returned to a life of imprisonment!" she declared.

"*You* were in prison?" Jake asked.

This time, Queen Elizabeth banged her cotton-swab scepter right on Jake's hand. "Yes, in the Tower of London whilst our sister, Mary, ruled as queen. She suspected us—wrongly, of course—of treasonous schemes," she replied impatiently. "Your ignorance pains us. It would behoove you to learn a little something of your queen and your country."

Not my queen or *my country*, Jake thought. Since he didn't want to set off another royal tantrum, he kept quiet. Besides, the last thing Jake had time for right now was learning about Queen Elizabeth. *Julia* had wished for her; she was *Julia's* problem. He had to get Mr. Chavez back to Franklin Field before it got too late.

"We are *known* for walking amongst our people," Queen Elizabeth was saying. "We are *loved* for it."

"Fine! We'll all go." Jake gave in. He carefully placed Mr. Chavez and Queen Elizabeth in his backpack, then hurried downstairs to tell Mom the plan.

"*With* Julia?" she asked in surprise.

"Yeah, sure," Jake said, acting like it was the most normal thing in the world to take his baby sister to work on a school project with his best friend.

"No, I don't think so," Mom said.

"But, Mom—" Jake began.

"I'm very glad to see you two getting along so well," Mom said. "But Julia's too young to go places without an adult."

"Sorry, Jake," Julia replied. But he couldn't miss

the look of relief on her face. "Guess I have to stay home."

That's just great, Jake thought. Now he was stuck keeping *both* geniuses out of trouble!

By the time Jake reached Franklin Field, Emerson was pacing by their garden bed. "Dude! What took you so long?" he called.

"Complications," Jake muttered as he zipped open his backpack. "Emerson, I'd like to introduce Her Royal Highness, Queen Elizabeth, and Mr. Cesar Chavez. Mr. Chavez says he can help us."

Mr. Chavez scooped up a tiny handful of dirt and let it run through his fingers. "Good soil," he said, nodding approvingly. "That's worth more than you know. You can hardly grow anything in poor soil. Now, what about water?"

"We've got plenty of water," Jake assured him. "I mean, it's kind of a pain to lug the watering cans across the field from school, but we can handle it."

"Good," Mr. Chavez replied. "On a farm, water can be the difference between life and death. I grew up on a beautiful ranch in Arizona, where my family grew corn and watermelon and squash. We kept chickens. But when a terrible drought struck, we lost everything."

"Everything?" Jake repeated in a quiet voice. It was hard to comprehend how horrible that would be.

"We weren't the only ones," Mr. Chavez continued. "It didn't help that we were in the middle of the Great Depression, a time when millions of Americans were too poor to even afford food. Many people suffered. For a lot of us, there was no choice but to move—to migrate—to a new place. Our very survival depended on it."

"Leave their homes?" Queen Elizabeth asked in surprise. "We would not allow our people to suffer so. When the harvest fails, it is our duty to help those in need."

"Where did you go?" Emerson asked Mr. Chavez.

"California," Mr. Chavez replied. "The Golden State . . . the Land of Milk and Honey . . . the Grape State. It's had a lot of nicknames over the years. My family went there because more food is grown in California than in any other state in the country. What we didn't realize was that the people who harvested that food would be treated so poorly."

"Are you playing with *dolls*?"

Jake froze.

There was no mistaking Aiden's voice.

Why? Jake thought frantically. *Why is he still at school? Practice ended ages ago.*

Queen Elizabeth and Mr. Chavez were standing right there—right in the dirt—and if they moved even a fraction of an inch, Aiden would see, Aiden would *know*—

Jake spun around and came face-to-face with Aiden.

Aiden's laugh rang across the field. "That makes way more sense," he said. "Because at first I thought you guys were actually working on your project, but then I was like, 'Everfail? Working on *anything*? Not a chance.' So I had to come see for myself."

"So you saw. Now you can leave," Emerson snapped.

"It's a free country," Aiden sneered as he knelt next to the garden bed. "Who do we have here, anyway? Oh, man, is this a *queen* doll?"

Jake stared at the ground. The momentary relief he felt when he realized Mr. Chavez and Queen Elizabeth had frozen in place faded as Jake tried to come up with an excuse. "It's not mine," he finally said. "It's my sister's."

"Yeah? Where is she?" Aiden asked. It was clear he was enjoying every minute of Jake's agony.

"At home," Jake choked out.

"Tsk, tsk," Aiden said. "That wasn't very nice to take your sister's dolls, Jake. But you know what? Since you're here, do you think you could give me some baseball advice?"

Jake's shoulders jerked up in a quick shrug. He didn't know exactly what Aiden was getting at, but he was pretty sure it wasn't really about baseball.

"I've been working on my throw," Aiden said. "I want to pitch when we play the Piranhas. How's my form?"

In one fast motion, Aiden scooped up Queen Elizabeth and threw her as hard as he could. Her fancy gown was a blur of color against the blue sky as she flew through the air.

Then Queen Elizabeth plunged to the ground.

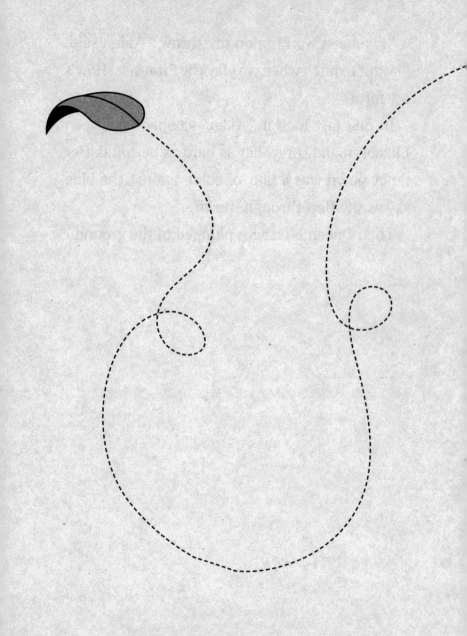

CHAPTER 5

Aiden's mocking laugh chased Jake across the field as he ran after Queen Elizabeth. As Jake stomped through the tall grasses beyond the school grounds, a terrible thought struck him: What if Aiden had thrown Queen Elizabeth *back* into the Wishing Well?

Not possible, Jake thought. *Aiden's aim is* definitely *not that good.*

But Jake didn't feel like he could take a full

breath until he finally located Queen Elizabeth, nearly hidden among the weeds and wildflowers.

"Your Highness!" Jake gasped, breathless. "Are you okay?"

"We have suffered a grievous assault on our dignity, but are otherwise unharmed," she replied with a haughty sniff as she brushed mud and grass from her gown. "The ranks of our sworn enemies have grown. Who was that scalawag?"

"Don't worry, he's my enemy, not yours," Jake said with a sigh.

"He's my enemy now," the queen said, narrowing her eyes as a look of grim determination settled over her face. Queen Elizabeth's stark white makeup was like a mask, hiding her true feelings. But as the sun started to set, Jake could see a glimpse of the person behind the crown.

"I'm so sorry Aiden did that to you," Jake said. "He's the worst."

Queen Elizabeth laughed. "Him? He's nothing," she said. "We've counted among our enemies our own half sister, Mary, and our most trusted friend, the Earl of Essex. Even the King of Spain tried to overthrow us. We repaid him by destroying his armada."

"Yikes," Jake said.

"We ushered in an age of peace and plenty for our beloved England. Yet there is no shortage of those who would doubt our abilities—or even our right to rule as queen," the monarch said, staring into the distance. Then she turned to Jake. "This Aiden chap is but a flea whose bites are bothersome, and nothing more. One word to our advisors on the Privy Council, and he'd soon be cut down to size."

I wish it could be that easy, Jake thought glumly. He didn't think even the Privy Council could stop Aiden's awfulness.

By the time Jake and Queen Elizabeth returned to the garden bed, Aiden was gone and Emerson was pacing again. "My parents will be so mad if I'm not home, like, five minutes ago," he said.

"Mine, too." Jake groaned. "This trip was a total waste of time—all because of Aiden."

"Not a total waste," Emerson told him. "Mr. Chavez gave me some tips while you were, uh, rescuing Queen Elizabeth."

"*We* were not in need of *rescue*," the Queen retorted.

"Right. My bad," Emerson said. "I mean, I'm sorry, Your Majesty."

With Mr. Chavez's expert advice, Jake and Emerson were able to make a plan for their garden bed. They learned all about which plants grew better together and which plants should be kept apart, a technique called companion planting. They even made charts so that each seed would be planted according to the proper spacing. When it was time for the class to plant, Jake and Emerson knew exactly what to do.

Jake dropped his final seed into the dirt and gently scooped some soil over it. Then he glanced up at Ms. Turner. "That's it?" he asked.

"That's it," she replied.

"What do we do now?" Emerson asked.

Ms. Turner smiled. "Water . . . and wait," she said. "If all goes well, you should see sprouts in a few days."

Jake stared into the dirt. It was hard to believe that those tiny, dry seeds would grow into plants that would feed people.

"From here on, we'll check the garden a couple of times a week during class time," Ms. Turner announced to the class. "You'll be responsible for taking care of the garden outside of school hours. Watering, pulling weeds, watching out for bugs that would eat your plants: Caring for the garden is now part of your homework."

A few days later, Jake and Emerson decided to check their garden before school. They were several feet away when Jake tilted his head and squinted. "Hey," he began. "Is that . . ."

"Sprouts!" Emerson hollered. "The seeds! They sprouted!"

The boys ran up to the garden, where the dark brown dirt was now speckled with bright pops of green. Seedlings! During the night, dozens of tiny green shoots had broken through the soil. As Jake knelt close to the dirt, he noticed that each shoot had a pair of leaves that had just started to unfurl. Jake and Emerson couldn't wait to tell *everyone*!

"It happened!" Jake yelled excitedly as he burst into the classroom. "We've got seedlings!"

"Aww, is Baby Jake excited about his baby plants?" Aiden mocked him.

At least the other students seemed more interested in Jake's news than in Aiden's latest insult. "Was it every seed you planted? Or just some?" Hannah asked eagerly.

"Who cares?" Aiden scoffed. "Seeds grow. Jake didn't do anything special."

But the rest of the class didn't agree. They ran over to the window, eager to get a look.

"I can't see anything," Hannah reported.

"The seedlings are pretty tiny," Jake told them. "They're hard to see unless you get up close."

"Do we have time to check our gardens before

the bell rings?" asked Marco, glancing at the clock.

"Not unless you want to get a tardy," Ms. Turner's voice carried over from the doorway. "Do I take it that there have been developments in the garden?"

"Jake and Emerson's seeds sprouted!" Clara exclaimed.

"Wonderful!" Ms. Turner replied. "I expect there will be lots of updates to your garden journals today. But first, it's just about time for morning announcements."

As if on cue, the bell rang. Jake hurried to his seat—but not without one last glance out the window at the Franklin Elementary Vegetable Garden, where incredible things were happening.

That night, Jake couldn't wait to tell his whole family about the seedlings. Julia, though, was late for dinner. Really late.

"Julia!" Mom called again. "We're waiting!"

"What's keeping her?" Dad asked.

Thump-clomp. Thump-clomp. Thump-clomp.

First they heard Julia, thunking down the stairs in Mom's too-big high heels.

Then they smelled her. It was like she'd gone swimming in a pool filled with perfume.

Finally, they saw her, wearing her fanciest dress, all of her costume jewelry, and enough makeup to look like a clown from the circus.

"What happened to you?" Jake asked in astonishment. He didn't need an answer, though. He could recognize Queen Elizabeth's influence— even if Julia had taken things a little too far.

"Does no one dress for dinner anymore?" Julia asked with a pained sigh. "Why have we become so coarse and uncoot?"

"Uncouth?" Dad guessed.

"That's what I said," Julia said, frowning.

Jake coughed to cover his laughter. Even Mom and Dad had to hide their smiles.

"So, kids, how was school today?" Mom asked.

"You'll never believe what happened in the garden!" Jake began. "There was nothing there yesterday—*nothing*. And now the bed is full of seedlings that will grow into plants that will make food that will actually feed people!"

Mom and Dad exchanged a smile across the table. "Wow! I bet you were surprised," Mom said.

Jake poked his fork into his salad and speared a piece of lettuce, a chunk of carrot, and a cherry tomato. "Just look at this," he said, waving his fork around. "All of this food was *grown* from the dirt. Somebody planted it and somebody harvested it, all so we could eat it!"

"Whoa!" Dad said as the cherry tomato fell off Jake's fork and rolled across the table. He nabbed it just before it fell into Flapjack's mouth.

"Your enthusiasm is great, champ," Dad continued. "You know, we've got some plants growing right in the backyard. Millions of blades of grass, in fact . . . if you ever want to take the lawn mower out and spend some quality time with them . . ."

Jake glanced out the window. "Why *do* we have so much grass planted out back?" he asked his parents. "We could totally grow some food for the food bank! Can we build some raised beds, Dad? Or—"

BANG! Julia slammed her fork onto the table.

"We have grown tired of this topic," she announced. "We would rather discuss our Funny Bunny collection."

"Julia, what's gotten into you?" Mom asked. "That wasn't very polite. Please apologize for interrupting Jake."

"Jake should apologize for boring us!" Julia replied.

"Young lady," Dad said. "Keep it up and I'll confiscate your Funny Bunnies until you can remember your manners."

"That's *Lady Julia*," she muttered—but quiet enough that only Jake heard her. Then Julia turned to Jake and said, "Sorry."

"It's okay," Jake replied—but inside, he wasn't so sure. Julia had been spending a lot of time with Queen Elizabeth.

Maybe a little *too* much time!

CHAPTER 6

Jake stared at his reflection in the mirror. It had been a while since he'd worn his Franklin Turkeys uniform. He never felt prouder than when he put on his aqua-and-purple jersey with the big white 7 on the back. Today, though, the jumble of emotions swirling inside of Jake was harder to describe: a mix of nervousness and excitement and worry and anticipation.

Would he play his best?

Would he make everyone proud?

Would the Turkeys win?

Soon, Jake would know the answer to those questions—and so would the whole town. It was time for the big game at last.

Dad was more chatty than usual as he drove Jake to the game. "Don't be nervous," he said. "You're going to do great."

"Mmm," Jake said, staring out the window. He didn't mean to tune Dad out. But he could already see some of his teammates warming up on the field.

"Remember, it's not whether you win or lose," Dad began.

"But how you play the game," Jake replied on cue. They always recited that famous saying before a game; it was an Everdale family tradition.

"Go get 'em, champ," Dad said with a grin.

"Thanks, Dad," Jake replied.

As Jake approached the dugout, he spotted Aiden strutting around like he owned the field.

Jake immediately pushed the unkind thought from his mind. Like it or not, Aiden was Jake's teammate now. They were on the same side, and that, Jake knew, was all that mattered—for today, at least.

Emerson jogged over. "Lucky socks?" he asked as he pointed at Jake's feet.

"Of course," Jake replied. As if he'd play in the big game *without* his lucky socks!

Emerson breathed a sigh of relief. "That's good," he said, jerking his thumb toward the Pinehurst Piranhas, who had just arrived. "I think we're going to need all the luck we can get."

Jake's eyes bugged out as the Piranhas marched across the parking lot. They looked determined— like they'd been spending every spare moment getting ready for this game.

That was all it took for Jake to get into the baseball zone. In the classroom, it was easy to get distracted when Ms. Turner was explaining magnets or the metric system. On the field, though, baseball captured his complete attention.

Jake glanced nervously at the batting order. He liked to bat early, when it mattered less if he struck out. There was too much pressure going up to bat when the bases were loaded or there were already a couple of outs.

I'm batting fourth! Jake realized. *Coach has me hitting cleanup?*

Now the pressure was really on.

As soon as the first pitch was thrown, Jake realized his instinct about the Piranhas was right: They were playing to win. But so were the Turkeys. And it turned out that the teams were surprisingly well matched. The innings zipped by, a blur of strikes and outs that didn't do much to move the scoreboard.

At the end of the first inning, the score was 1–0 Piranhas.

At the top of the fourth, it was 1–2 Turkeys.

By the sixth inning, the teams were tied, 2–2. The Turkeys were up to bat. They'd either win the game or send it to extra innings.

Jake picked up his favorite bat and took a

couple of warm-up swings. Then he heard something odd. The Piranhas were chanting in low, steady unison, but Jake couldn't quite recognize the words. It sounded like they were saying, "Maybe! Maybe! Maybe!"

Maybe what? Jake wondered. *Maybe they think I'll strike out?*

The Piranhas were still chanting as Jake approached home plate. As he got into position, adjusting his stance a little, the voices grew louder. And that's when Jake realized with sickening clarity that they weren't chanting "maybe" at all.

They were chanting "baby."

"Baby! Baby! Baby!"

Aiden, Jake thought. He didn't need to turn around to see Aiden smirking at him from the dugout. How pleased he must be. How proud of his plan to mess with Jake's head right when he needed to focus more than ever.

What kind of person does that to his teammate? Jake wondered, clenching the bat even tighter. Something surged through Jake—not a feeling of anger, exactly, but of *power*. Then the weirdest thing happened. Jake knew the Piranhas were still chanting "baby," but he couldn't hear them anymore, not really. His other senses diminished until his only focus was watching the ball, cupped in the pitcher's hand.

When the pitch came, Jake was ready for it. He was more than ready.

Thwack!

A clean, clear *crack* rang through the air. The bat met the ball at just the right speed and angle, making the impact vibrate into Jake's hands and up his arms. He knew it was a good hit—he could *feel* it—but he didn't waste a moment wondering how good, or where the ball was flying.

All he did was run along the baseline.

Run-run-run-run-run *bam!* his foot on first base run-run-run-run-run *bam!* his foot on second base run-run-run-run-run—

Will I make it home? Jake wondered wildly. A home run—that would be so—it would be—

Bam!

Jake was rounding third.

The crowd was screaming.

There was one last baseline to run.

One last base to hit.

Somewhere the ball was being tossed from Piranha to Piranha, moving ever closer to tag him out, but Jake pushed himself even harder. He would be faster, he would be stronger, he would be unstoppable!

Jake's foot hit home plate like it was a launchpad, sending him into the stratosphere.

A home run, Jake thought, dizzy with glee.

He was breathing hard and smiling even harder. As his teammates rushed onto the field to celebrate with him, Jake thought that he heard Mom and Dad and Julia screaming his name in the crowd. How many times had he imagined a win like this before shaking the thought away as a silly daydream?

The truth, though, was that no daydream could compare to the incredible reality. It couldn't even come close.

The Franklin Turkeys were the winners—and it was all thanks to Jake!

Jake and Emerson were still in celebration mode when they walked to school on Monday. At the main entrance, the boys were greeted by a banner that read CHAMPION TURKEYS in bright letters. A crowd had formed to celebrate the return of the golden dog bowl, and every student and teacher they saw wanted to congratulate Jake and Emerson on the Turkeys' big win.

The boys' good moods lasted all day—until it was time for their class to check on the garden beds.

"Oh no!" Emerson exclaimed, frowning down at their raised bed. The seedlings hadn't grown at all! In fact, they looked shriveled and sickly, drooping in the dirt.

Jake stared at the garden in dismay. "What happened?" he asked.

"I don't know! They look dead! Are they all dying?" Emerson replied.

"I wish Mr. Chavez was here," Jake said. "He'd know what's wrong with them."

"Poor plants," Emerson said. "I can't believe I feel this sad about it. They're just plants. But they look so pitiful."

They flagged down Ms. Turner to take a look. Even she was surprised by the appearance of the seedlings.

"Have you been watering them?" she asked.

"Every other day," Emerson told her. "But . . . not over the weekend. With the game and everything . . ."

"That's okay," she said. "Two days without water wouldn't cause this. I can't imagine what happened to them. The leaves almost look burned."

"What should we do?" Jake asked.

Ms. Turner thought about it for a moment. "Give them a really good watering," she suggested. "Make sure the soil is wet throughout, just in case the water hasn't been reaching the roots."

"Then what?" Emerson said.

"Then we wait and see," she replied. "Maybe they'll bounce back."

"But what if they don't?" Jake asked.

"Well, you might have to start over," Ms. Turner said. "Hopefully it won't come to that."

"Here, Jake," Clara said. "Do you and Emerson want to use our watering can?"

"Thanks," Jake replied. As he grabbed the can, he realized that Aiden was watching him. He had the same look on his face that Jake had seen so many times before—a mix of meanness and satisfaction—and now something else, too.

Happiness.

And that's when the thought struck Jake, as shocking and unexpected as a bolt of lightning in a cloudless sky: *What if* Aiden *had done something to their garden?*

CHAPTER 7

After school, Jake and Emerson ran to Jake's room without even stopping for a snack. They found Queen Elizabeth in the middle of giving Julia a dancing lesson.

Queen Elizabeth stamped her foot. "We hope that the matter is one of urgent necessity," she said. "We cannot imagine that you would dare interrupt us for any lesser reason."

"It's our mutual enemy," Jake said, breathless. "He's—he's been plotting."

"Say no more," the queen declared. Then she turned to Julia. "We shall continue this anon."

"Anonymously?" Emerson asked, confused. "Is Julia's dancing that bad?"

"It is *not*," Julia said, highly insulted. "She means *later*!"

"Mr. Chavez, would you take a look at our plants?" Jake asked. "I think someone tampered with our garden."

"Of course," Mr. Chavez replied. "But who would do such a thing?"

As they hurried to Franklin Elementary, Jake let himself feel hopeful. Maybe the plants really were under-watered. Maybe the cans of water that he and Emerson had lugged over would be enough to refresh them.

But Jake's hopes faded as they approached the garden bed. The plants looked even worse. Puny and pitiful, all the seedlings had collapsed onto the still-damp soil.

One look at Mr. Chavez's face confirmed their suspicions. The seedlings were doomed.

"Isn't there anything we can do?" Jake asked.

"Start over," Mr. Chavez said. "But it would help if we could discover the reason for the crop's failure."

"They were growing so well," Jake said, shaking his head. "I just don't understand."

"Salt," Queen Elizabeth said suddenly. "This is a declaration of war!"

"Say what?" asked Emerson.

"In ancient times, conquerors would salt the fields of their vanquished enemies so that no crops would grow," Mr. Chavez explained. "I can't say if that's what happened here. But it's certainly possible. A plant in salted soil can't take up the water it needs. It withers and dies, as if no water was offered."

Jake buried his head in his hands. "I never wanted a war with Aiden," he said miserably. "I just wanted to grow some food for the food bank and not fail the project!"

"Don't despair," Mr. Chavez told him. "I have seen justice prevail despite impossible odds. The grape boycott, for example."

Jake looked up. "What happened?" he asked.

"The grape growers were so powerful. They wouldn't pay a fair wage, while the workers toiled in terrible conditions," he explained. "To change anything, the workers had to strike together. And the strike, which lasted nearly five years, was just the beginning. We marched three hundred miles. I refused to eat for twenty-five days to bring attention to the cause. And, slowly, families across the United States started paying attention. They joined our cause by boycotting, or refusing to buy, grapes.

"With no one to harvest the grapes, they withered on the vines," Mr. Chavez continued. "With no one to buy them, they rotted in the stores. The grape growers finally had no choice but to meet our demands. We showed the world that when the people are united, anything is possible."

"Wow," Jake said. "This is just me, though. And Emerson now, I guess. We can't exactly lead a boycott of Aiden."

"Still, you can stand up," Mr. Chavez told him. "Si, se puede."

"What does that mean?" Jake asked.

Mr. Chavez smiled. "Si, se puede is a rallying cry for anyone who would stand against injustice. The closest translation would be 'yes, we can,'" he said. "And you can do it, Jake. I believe in you."

"I don't know how," Jake replied. "I don't know where to start."

"You yourself are reason enough to take a stand," Mr. Chavez said. "But if you cannot take a stand for yourself, you must find the courage to do it for others."

"For others?" Jake repeated.

Mr. Chavez nodded. "I've never known a bully who was content to have one target," he said. "It may not be today—or tomorrow—but if this young man continues unchecked . . ."

Mr. Chavez didn't need to finish his sentence. Jake understood. And he understood what he needed to do next. But there were still unanswered questions that nagged at him.

"So if I stand up to Aiden . . . what happens next?" Jake asked. "If I tell him to cut it out, he'll just laugh in my face. Am I supposed to fight him?"

Just saying the words made Jake feel sick.

Mr. Chavez held up his hands. "No. Never! There are better ways of righting wrongs," he said. "If you fight Aiden, you will cede the higher ground."

"Maybe you should tell Ms. Turner," Emerson said.

"That would just make me a tattletale," Jake said, shaking his head. "Besides, I don't have any proof. Who would believe me? Aiden's never gotten in trouble for anything. And I get in trouble all the time."

"We would enlist our network of spies," Queen Elizabeth said. "When foul plots are brewing, there is always evidence to be found. Then our guards would capture the traitor and imprison him in the Tower of London to await execution."

"Execution?" Jake gulped.

"Beheading!" the queen said cheerfully.

Jake shook his head again. "I'm sorry, Your Majesty," he said. "But we have laws about that kind of thing."

"Pity," Queen Elizabeth replied.

"Spies," Emerson said suddenly.

Jake gave him a look. "Pretty sure we have laws about that, too, dude," he said.

"No, listen up," Emerson said. He turned to Queen Elizabeth. "Your spies gather evidence?"

"Indeed, they do," she replied.

"So that's what we need to do," Emerson told Jake. "Not spies, though—*us*."

"But how?" Jake asked. "Aiden is too smart. He'll never mess with our garden when we're around."

"Not when we're around, no," Emerson said. "But if he doesn't *know* we're there . . . like if we're hiding out near the Wishing Well . . ."

"Go on," Jake encouraged him.

"With a camera . . . or a cell phone . . ." Emerson said. "And if Aiden shows up and messes with our garden bed . . ."

"We'd have our proof," Jake said. He looked over at Mr. Chavez and Queen Elizabeth. "What do you think?"

"It's a plan worthy of the Privy Council," Queen Elizabeth said. "Catch the traitor in the vile act of treachery so that there will be no doubt!"

"The question is—once you have proof, what will you do with it?" Mr. Chavez asked.

And that was a question Jake couldn't answer.

At least, not yet.

That very afternoon, Jake and Emerson planted a new batch of seeds. They watched and waited, checking their garden twice a day—but after more than a week, none of the seeds had sprouted.

"There's got to be something wrong with the soil," Emerson insisted. He tapped a page in his garden journal. "See this? Last time we had sprouts after four days! And now—nothing!"

"Okay," Jake replied with a sigh. "Let's talk to Ms. Turner."

At recess, Jake and Emerson stayed behind.

"How can I help you, boys?" Ms. Turner asked.

"We're worried about our garden," Jake began. "Our new seeds haven't even sprouted."

"Hmm," Ms. Turner said. "Let's see your journals."

Jake and Emerson were quiet while she flipped through the pages. At last, Ms. Turner looked up. "You're doing everything right, from what I can tell," she said. "What do you think the problem is?"

"Maybe the soil?" Emerson said.

"If there's something wrong with our soil, then it would explain why our garden keeps failing," Jake added. He tried not to think of all the other garden beds, filled with thick and healthy plants.

"We were thinking we could get some new dirt over the weekend," Emerson said.

"I can't imagine it's the dirt," Ms. Turner said, shaking her head. "Everyone used the same soil."

Emerson and Jake exchanged a glance.

"But if you think it would help, it's fine with me," Ms. Turner continued.

Yes! Jake thought as relief washed over him. Now it was time for the second request.

"Could we start some seeds at home?" Jake said in a rush. "Otherwise we'll fall even farther behind."

"I don't see why not," Ms. Turner replied. "You've already had the chance to plant directly in the dirt. Maybe starting seeds at home then transferring them into new soil will do the trick."

"Thank you," Emerson said. "We really don't want to fail this project."

Ms. Turner smiled at the boys. "I know how hard you're working," she assured them. "Now, if you hurry, you might be able to have some fun at recess before the bell rings."

There were so many thoughts bouncing around Jake's brain that he didn't even care about missing recess.

"Want to come over after school so we can plant seeds?" Emerson asked.

"Sounds good," Jake said.

"We're gonna have the best garden!" Emerson said. "We're gonna baby our plants like they're actual babies! Our seedlings are gonna grow so big and strong. When we bring them to school, everyone—"

Emerson sucked in his breath sharply.

"What is it?" Jake asked.

"What do you think would happen," Emerson began, "if we brought a bunch of awesome, healthy seedlings to school? Like, we march into class with them and make a big scene?"

"Everybody would gather around to look," Jake replied. "Ms. Turner would be excited. And Aiden would . . ."

There were so many ways to fill in the blank. Jake had plenty of experience with how Aiden reacted whenever things were going well for him—and it was never good. What might Aiden do this time? Especially if he thought no one was watching?

Jake had a feeling they were going to find out.

CHAPTER 8

For the next two weeks, Jake and Emerson dedicated every spare moment to their farm project. They spent hours removing the old dirt from their garden bed and replacing it with fresh dirt from the garden supply store. They planted new seeds at home and watched them sprout. Every day, they tended their seedlings, misting the young plants with spray bottles and bringing them inside if it seemed like it might get too cold overnight. When it was finally time to bring the sprouts to school, Jake's heart pounded like he was marching to his doom.

"We could just leave the plants outside," Jake said as they approached the school entrance. "We don't have to take them to the classroom first and make a big deal of it, when that will definitely make Aiden mad."

Emerson shook his head. "No way. I'm *proud* of these little guys!" he said, gesturing to the seedlings. "We worked *really* hard to grow them. I want Ms. Turner to know. I want everyone to know!"

"That's easy for you to say," Jake said. "Aiden doesn't hate you like he hates me. He's always *watching*—he's always ready to—"

"I know, dude," Emerson said, and his voice was suddenly softer than Jake had ever heard him before.

"So maybe let's not give him a reason to come after us!" Jake exclaimed.

"But we're *not* giving him a reason," Emerson insisted. "We're just being us. You have a right to be at Franklin Elementary, Jake! And play base-ball, and do good at school, and have friends, and, like, everything else that Aiden is always trying to take from you."

Jake knew Emerson wouldn't care if the tears in his eyes leaked out, but he stared straight ahead anyway and willed himself not to cry. It was the first time anyone had described what it was like to live in the shadow of Aiden's unkind-ness. He felt like a used-up eraser on the end of a pencil.

"Maybe we're wrong and Aiden hasn't been sabotaging our project," Emerson continued. "But if he has—and if he tries it again . . ." He paused and zipped open his backpack. When Jake peeked in, he saw Mr. Lewis's video camera wrapped in one of Emerson's sweatshirts. "We'll be ready for him!"

When they reached Ms. Turner's class, Emerson strode through the door as Jake trailed behind him.

"Behold, the wonders of nature!" Emerson

announced. "The Plant Masters are reporting for duty!"

Everyone started to laugh as Emerson did a funny dance toward Ms. Turner's desk.

"Plant Masters—or Dance Masters?" Ms. Turner asked with a smile. "Your seedlings look great! I hope this fresh start is just what your garden needs to thrive. Marco, Hannah, let's make some room on the windowsill. We'll put Jake and Emerson's seedlings there until gardening time this afternoon."

"Soakin' up some extra sun," Emerson sang as he danced the seedlings over to the window.

Everyone laughed again, even Jake.

Well, almost everyone.

Jake glanced over at just the right moment to catch a glimpse of Aiden's face. His eyes were narrowed, focusing with laser-like intensity on Jake.

Maybe Jake should have felt worried. Maybe he should have felt afraid. But Queen Elizabeth's words came back to him: *This Aiden chap is but a flea whose bites are bothersome, and nothing more.*

Jake straightened his shoulders and found a secret source of determination that he didn't even know he had. Then Jake caught Emerson's eye and nodded, just once. Emerson, who knew exactly what Jake meant, nodded in response.

It's on.

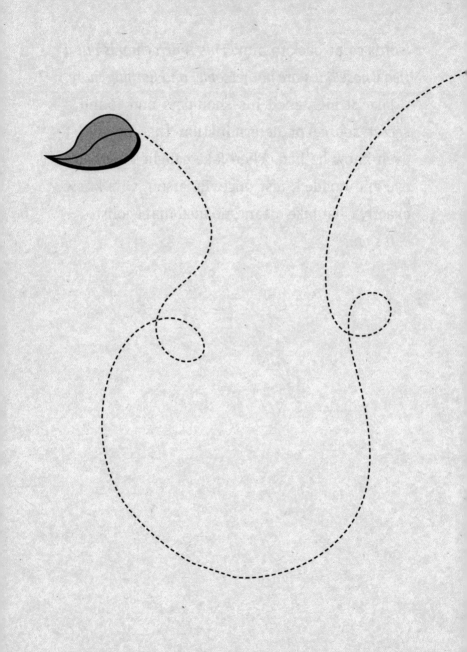

CHAPTER 9

After school, Jake and Emerson started their walk home like it was any other day. But instead of turning left on Oak Street, they looped all the way around Franklin Woods. Then, with a careful glance to make sure no one was looking, they slipped through the trees.

"Watch out for poison ivy," Emerson said in a low voice.

"Thanks," Jake replied—but poison ivy was the least of his worries. Jake still hadn't figured out what, exactly, he would do if they caught Aiden messing with their garden bed. Every time Jake tried to imagine what it would be like, his brain shut it down. The whole thing seemed too impossible to be true. After all, what was more likely—that all-As Aiden was sabotaging Jake's project?

Or that Jake "Everfail" was just doing what he did best—fail?

After several minutes, the boys reached the other side of the woods. It was odd to look at Franklin Elementary from here. The brick building seemed both smaller and farther away than it really was.

Emerson glanced around, then moved behind a large bush. "I don't think he'll be able to see us if we hide here," he said. "Check it out."

Jake crouched next to Emerson. He had to admit it was the perfect hiding place. Through the branches, Jake had a clear view of the garden beds. The leaves were thick enough that if Jake sat very still, no one would notice him.

Emerson plunked down next to Jake and started messing with his dad's camera. The boys were so quiet that Jake could hear the water rushing through the storm drain—the Wishing Well—nearby. *Too bad I already used my wish,* Jake thought. Maybe he should have wished that Aiden would stop picking on him. Sure, he probably would've failed everything and gotten kicked off the team—but right now, that almost seemed like the better option.

"So . . . what now?" Jake finally asked.

"Now we wait," Emerson said. He never looked away from the garden beds—not even for a moment.

The seconds ticked away, stretching into minutes as Jake tried not to fidget. Jake wondered how much time had passed. He wished he could sneak a glance at the flashing red numbers of the clock in Ms. Turner's classroom.

At last, Jake didn't think he could sit still for

one more second. "This is a waste of time," he said as he started to stand up. "Let's go—"

"Shhhh!" Emerson hissed. He grabbed Jake's wrist and pulled him down.

Jake fell to the ground with a thud. He stared through the branches. And there it was: a lone figure leaving Franklin Elementary School and crossing the field.

"It's Aiden," Emerson whispered.

Jake held his breath as Aiden reached the garden. He walked slowly around the beds, pausing by his own. Then Aiden started walking again, staring into each garden bed as he passed it.

What's he doing? Jake wondered, frowning. *It's like he's looking for something. But . . . what?*

Then Aiden stopped.

Stopped right next to Jake and Emerson's bed, where they had planted all their strong, thriving seedlings just hours before.

Jake's breath caught in his throat. He could feel

Emerson's shoulders stiffen beside him, but Jake didn't dare look away from the garden.

Aiden glanced around—to the left, to the right, to the left again.

Then he knelt in the dirt and reached into his backpack.

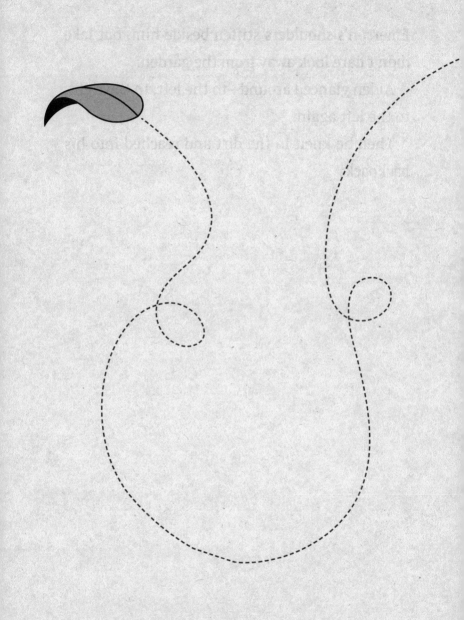

CHAPTER 10

Jake blinked. He didn't want to believe it, but there was no denying that Aiden was about to do *something* to Jake and Emerson's garden bed. A hot wave of anger swelled in Jake's chest as he thought about their first crop of seedlings that had suddenly pitched over and died.

So much work, so much time, all wasted—

And here was Aiden, about to do it again—

That's when Jake remembered what Mr. Chavez had said: *If you cannot take a stand for yourself, you must find the courage to do it for others.*

The problems with Aiden had only gotten worse, week after week, month after month. Aiden's hatred had already taken so much from Jake. And now it had taken the food that Jake and Emerson could have grown for hungry families. Jake knew what he had to do. He crashed through the bushes, not caring about the noise or the thorns or the sound of Emerson urgently calling his name.

"Aiden! Stop!" Jake yelled in a voice he barely recognized.

Aiden spun around. His hands were fumbling as he shoved something into his backpack. All Jake could think was that he had to get it, he *had* to get it away from Aiden before he could—

"Get *off*," Aiden snarled as Jake's hand wrapped around the strap of Aiden's backpack. He jerked his backpack, but Jake wouldn't let go; not for anything.

Aiden pulled harder on the backpack. Jake dug in his heels and held on with all his might.

"Since when do you care about your grades, Everfail?" Aiden sneered. "Failing is the only thing you do better than anyone else."

"It wasn't just a grade!" Jake exploded. "Those plants were gonna feed people! And you killed them all!"

There was a brief flicker in Aiden's eyes—a moment of doubt, maybe, or remorse. Or maybe Jake imagined it, because suddenly Aiden was pulling even harder on his backpack. "Let go, loser!" he yelled.

"No," Jake said. Because he wasn't a loser. He wasn't a failure. And he was going to stand up for himself for once.

The backpack jerked back and forth between the boys, like the most important game of tug-of-war Franklin Field had ever seen. Jake wasn't going to give up, and neither was Aiden.

In the end, though, the backpack couldn't take it.

There was a loud *rrrrrrip*, and suddenly Jake found himself flying backwards, still holding on to the torn strap of Aiden's backpack. A hard landing knocked the wind out of him. Jake spent a moment catching his breath before he scrambled to his feet.

Across the grass, Aiden was doing the same thing. He looked at his ripped backpack, then charged toward Jake. Jake took a quick step to the side, and just like that they were circling each other warily.

"Hey! Both of you—stop! Now!"

A man's voice echoed across the field.

Jake's head swung to the side so fast that everything looked blurry. When his eyes focused again, he saw it: Mr. Pelman, running across the field. How much had he seen? How much did he know?

"Break it up!" Mr. Pelman yelled. It was only seconds until he was standing between the two boys. "What's going on?"

Jake opened his mouth and closed it and opened it again. He didn't know where to begin.

"Jake ripped my backpack," Aiden said.

"That's not—" Jake began.

"It is! Look! You can see it right there!" Aiden spoke over him, pointing at the torn strap.

Mr. Pelman held up a hand to quiet Aiden. "Jake?" he said. "What's going on?"

Jake took a deep breath. He wasn't sure what to say, until it suddenly hit him.

He would tell Mr. Pelman the truth.

"Aiden makes fun of me all the time," Jake began. "He's always calling me names. And he's been messing with our farm project. Our plants were doing great but he killed them all and now Aiden's out here trying to kill them again!"

"You liar!" Aiden yelled. "I would never do that!"

"So what's in your backpack?" Emerson asked.

Everyone turned to look as he emerged from the woods, still carrying the camera in his shaking hands.

Jake glanced at Aiden just in time to see a look of panic career across his face.

"That's—it's—that's none of your business," Aiden spat. In one fast move he pulled his backpack closer, cradling it against his chest.

"I filmed it all," Emerson said. "Aiden's got something in his backpack, and I'm pretty sure it's not plant food."

"Aiden," Mr. Pelman said in a quiet voice. "What's in your backpack?"

There was a long pause.

"Just—my stuff," Aiden said. "It's private. It's nobody's business."

Mr. Pelman nodded. "Okay," he said. "So, here's what we're going to do. We're going inside and I'm going to call your parents. *Everybody's* parents."

Jake swallowed hard. *Mom and Dad are going to be so mad at me*, he thought numbly.

"And then you can show your parents what's in your backpack," Mr. Pelman continued, staring at Aiden. "But I think I already know what's in there. I think it's the big box of salt that was recently stolen from the cafeteria. Am I right?"

The silence stretched and stretched.

And then the strangest thing happened. Aiden's shoulders slumped, and his head drooped down. Then, without another word, he handed the torn backpack to Mr. Pelman.

Everyone could see the box of salt right on top.

CHAPTER 11

It seemed like Jake and Emerson waited for ages in the hallway while Mr. Pelman spoke with Aiden. For once, they didn't have much to say to each other. Jake's stomach was clenched with worry. *The secret's out now,* he thought. If Aiden got into trouble, he'd never forgive Jake. It would probably just inspire Aiden to think of all-new ways to make Jake's life miserable.

Plus, Mr. Pelman was going to call Mom and Dad. Jake dreaded the moment when they would appear at school—the looks on their faces—here he was, in trouble *again*—

"Jake?"

Jake jumped when Mr. Pelman called his name. Aiden was standing beside him, head bowed, cheeks blazing red.

"Sit there," Mr. Pelman told Aiden. Then, to Jake: "Come on in."

Jake stood up a little too fast, which made his stomach lurch. He was careful not to look at Aiden as they passed each other in the hall.

"Have a seat," Mr. Pelman told Jake as he sat down behind his desk. This wasn't the first time Jake had been called into Mr. Pelman's office. He grabbed one of the fidgeters on Mr. Pelman's desk and started to fiddle with it. The smooth metal in his hands was a welcome distraction from whatever Mr. Pelman was going to say.

But Mr. Pelman didn't speak. The silence lasted longer and longer until Jake finally looked at him.

"You ready?" asked Mr. Pelman.

"Ready for what?" Jake replied.

"To tell me what's been going on," Mr. Pelman said. "Whatever was happening out there in the garden—and I've got a pretty good idea—obviously didn't start today. In fact, I think it's been going on for quite a while. If I had to guess, you've been keeping it inside for a long time. You must be ready to burst, Jake."

Jake's head jerked up and down, but he still wasn't ready to talk. Not yet.

"Adults are always expecting kids to solve their own problems," Mr. Pelman continued. "We're always saying things like 'Work it out on your own' or 'Don't be a tattletale.' Too often, we forget that some problems are too big for kids to handle by themselves."

Jake looked up fast.

"So I understand why you haven't come to me

or Ms. Turner or Coach Carlson," Mr. Pelman said. "Maybe you thought we wouldn't care. But I care, Jake. And I'm here to listen—whenever you're ready to talk."

Jake squirmed a little in his chair. Should he or shouldn't he? Yes or no? *If I tell Mr. Pelman everything, Aiden will be so mad. Everything will get worse,* he worried.

Then Jake had a new thought. *But it's already getting worse,* he realized. *Maybe telling Mr. Pelman is the way to make it better.*

Jake wasn't sure what to say or where to begin. But when he opened his mouth, the words spilled out faster than a rushing waterfall.

Mr. Pelman was a good listener. He didn't interrupt, not even once. When Jake was finally finished, he flopped back in his chair and exhaled in a long, shuddery sigh. He hadn't realized how heavy it was to carry around so many worries about Aiden.

"I'm sorry," Mr. Pelman began. "There's a word for what Aiden has been doing to you. It's called 'bullying.' Repeated and persistent—that means it happens again and again—behavior that intimidates, threatens, or harms another person. And I'm sure you know that Franklin Elementary is a bully-free zone."

"But it's not," Jake spoke up, surprising himself.

"Go on," Mr. Pelman encouraged him.

"I mean, if Aiden was bullying me, then this school *isn't* bully free," Jake said. "And it's wrong to say it is."

Mr. Pelman nodded. "I see your point," he replied. "But what we mean is that we aren't going to tolerate bullying. We have rules about it—and plans for stopping it."

"So what happens next?" Jake asked.

"A few different things," Mr. Pelman began. "I'll be having a lot of conversations—with your parents and Aiden's parents; with Principal Barron and Ms. Turner and Coach Carlson. There will be a team of teachers who know what's going on so that they can pay extra-close attention to the way Aiden treats other students. Especially you.

"There are consequences to bullying that Aiden will have to face," Mr. Pelman continued. "But the most important part of what happens next is finding a way for you and Aiden to move forward and, I hope, work together to fix this."

"Me?" Jake asked. He wasn't expecting that.

"Yes—if you're willing," Mr. Pelman said. "That won't be for a while, though. This problem didn't start overnight, and we won't be able to fix it overnight. But I can promise you this: Aiden's bullying of you stops today. Not just today—it stops *now*."

A few days later, Mom and Dad had a conference with Mr. Pelman and Aiden's parents. Jake and Julia waited for them at the garden, along with Mr. Chavez and Queen Elizabeth.

"Not bad, huh?" Jake asked proudly. The plants that Jake and Emerson had transferred were thriving. Not only had they grown several inches but they were dotted with flowers, from itty-bitty blossoms on the tomato plants to delicate white blooms on the pea vines.

"So pretty!" Julia cried, leaning over to smell them.

"Not just pretty," Jake told her. "Those flowers are going to turn into real food—tomatoes and peas and zucchini and more! Right?"

"That's right," Mr. Chavez said, beaming. He walked through the garden, nodding approvingly at the strong, healthy plants. "You and Emerson are doing a fine job, Jake. I expect you'll have a bountiful harvest."

"I hope so," Jake said, thinking of the hungry families who would receive the food.

"And the other matter?" Queen Elizabeth asked pointedly.

"Aiden," Jake said. "It's . . ." His voice trailed off as he tried to figure out how to answer her. "Better? I think? Aiden pretty much ignores me now. But Mr. Pelman still wants us to sit down together and talk."

"Parley," Queen Elizabeth said, nodding. "There's no shame in peace talks after vanquishing your enemy."

"That's the thing," Jake said, struggling to explain. "Aiden's—well, he's not my enemy. Not anymore. I don't know *what* he is now. We're definitely not friends."

"But you can both come to the table," said Mr. Chavez. "Some of the best negotiations happen between those who thought they could never find common ground."

"We'll see," Jake replied.

"In the meantime, keep up the good work with your garden," Mr. Chavez said. "Don't forget to keep an eye out for weeds. You want to pull them before they spread. Like that dandelion there— look, it's gone to seed already."

Mr. Chavez strode across the garden bed to the fluffy white dandelion. When he yanked on the stem, the seeds trembled—but the stubborn roots didn't budge.

"Step aside," Queen Elizabeth declared as

she grabbed the stem, too. She and Mr. Chavez pulled together—pulled harder—pulled with all their might—

"I'll get it. I want to make a wish," Julia began.

Pop!

The dandelion sprang from the dirt at the same moment as a warm breeze swirled over the garden bed. It lifted the entire dandelion—and the geniuses—high into the air!

"Wait!" Jake scrambled to his feet. "I didn't get—"

He could already tell it was too late. The dandelion puff danced and twirled on the breeze, floating higher, higher, higher—

"Farewell, Jake! Good-bye, Lady Julia!" Queen Elizabeth's voice rang out.

"Never forget—*you yourself are reason enough*," Mr. Chavez said. His voice sounded hollow and far away.

Jake and Julia watched in silence until the dandelion and the geniuses were just a tiny speck in the clear blue sky. Then they disappeared completely.

"So—that's it?" Julia asked. "They're just—gone?"

"Yeah," Jake replied.

"I'm going to miss them," Julia said with a sigh. "Aren't you?"

"Sure, I guess," Jake said, still staring at the sky. "But it will also be kind of nice for things to get back to normal."

CHAPTER 12

At last, the day of the first harvest and family picnic arrived. Jake and Julia helped Mom load up the picnic basket. They had planned the perfect menu: peanut-butter-and-honey sandwiches, carrot sticks and hummus, strawberries, and snickerdoodle cookies.

"There's so much food in here we should probably drive," Dad joked.

"It's such a beautiful day," Mom said, shaking her head. "Let's walk."

"Hope those clouds stay away," Dad replied as he glanced up at the sky.

"Why are you bringing your backpack?" Jake asked Julia as they walked behind Mom and Dad. "It's not a school day."

Julia shrugged and looked away. "Oh, yeah," she said. "I guess I forgot. You know what else I forgot? How your Heroes of History came to life. You just threw them into the Wishing Well?"

Jake glanced at Mom and Dad to make sure they weren't listening. "Pretty much," he replied in a low voice. "I spun around three times and made my wish and the rest, I guess, is history."

"And that's it?" Julia said. "Nothing else?"

"Nope," Jake told her.

When they arrived at school, the party at the garden was just getting started. Picnic blankets were strewn around Franklin Field; some kids were playing ball while others blew bubbles.

Best of all, though, were the garden beds, which were crowded with bright green plants.

"Wow," Mom said, clearly impressed. "I'm not exactly sure what I was expecting, but this is really something!"

"How about a tour?" Dad suggested.

Jake grinned. "Right this way," he announced with a funny bow. Jake couldn't hide his pride as he led his family through the garden, pointing out all the different vegetables, from ripening tomatoes to the carrot tops just peeking out of the ground.

"And all this food will be donated to the food bank," Jake explained.

"Incredible!" Mom exclaimed. "Which garden bed is yours?"

"It's over here," Jake said, pointing. "Our plants aren't as big as the others because . . . well . . . you know."

"They're thriving, though," Ms. Turner said as she joined Jake and his family. "It's not a bad thing that your plants are behind the others, Jake. It will extend the harvest."

"Really?" Jake asked.

"Yes, after all the other plants have finished producing for the season, yours will still be going strong," she explained. "I know how hard you and Emerson have worked on this project. Despite disappointments and setbacks, you never gave up. You brainstormed different ideas to try, and you both did a lot of extra work. That's why I'm giving you an A-plus."

Jake opened his mouth, but no words came out. *An A-plus?* he thought. He'd never received an A-plus before.

"Way to go, champ!" Dad cheered as he clapped Jake on the shoulder.

"We're so proud of you," Mom told Jake, cupping her hand on his cheek. "And not just because of the A-plus."

"Seriously?" Jake asked in surprise. Mom and Dad had been obsessing about his schoolwork for years. And now that he'd finally gotten some good grades, that wasn't why they were proud?

"Your grades are just one part of who you are," Mom said. "We're proud of *all* the parts of Jake. The helpful teammate, the loyal friend, the great son, the awesome big brother . . ."

Suddenly, Mom stopped. "Where's Julia?" she asked.

"Uh," Jake began, glancing around. "She was just . . ."

Jake's voice trailed off as he realized that he didn't see Julia anywhere. "I *thought* she was right here," he finished.

"That's what I thought, too," Mom said. Her forehead was puckered with worry. "I'm going to check the school. Maybe she went to the bathroom."

"I'll look on the playground," Dad said.

Thunder rumbled overhead as Jake's parents hurried away. The storm clouds were moving fast. All over Franklin Field, families were packing up their picnics.

Julia hates storms, Jake thought, starting to worry.

"Dude!" Emerson yelled. "You're gonna get drenched. Let's get inside!"

"I'm looking for Julia," Jake said. "Have you seen her?"

"What? You sister is lost?" Emerson exclaimed. He glanced warily at the sky. "I'll help you find her."

"No, you go ahead," Jake told him. "Maybe she's already inside. I'll catch up soon."

Crack!

The bolt of lightning that ripped through the sky seemed to tear open the clouds. It wasn't just rain; it was an all-out downpour. People shrieked as they ran toward the school.

But Jake stood oddly still as the rain soaked his clothes. *It hasn't rained this hard in a while*, he thought, remembering another time he'd been caught in a storm on Franklin Field . . . or, rather, just beyond it . . .

"The Wishing Well," he whispered. And suddenly, it all made sense: Julia's probing questions about how, exactly, the Heroes of History had come to help him; her insistence on bringing her backpack even though it wasn't a school day . . .

Jake took off running for the woods as the rain fell harder. Just as he feared, there was a small figure crouched by the storm drain. It was Julia, and she was awfully close to the edge.

Too close.

"Julia!" Jake shouted. "Stop! What are you doing? Get away from there!"

Julia turned to look at him. "Jake!" she cried, her face shining with happiness. "I did it! I made my wish!"

AUTHOR'S NOTE

Queen Elizabeth I was born September 7, 1533, in Greenwich, England, the second daughter of Henry VIII. King Henry was so eager for a son to inherit the throne that he was disappointed when Elizabeth was a daughter. It was rare for girls to be educated during that time, but Elizabeth's status as a princess gave her the opportunity for an excellent education. No one knew it at the time, but these lessons prepared her to become one of the most powerful people in the world.

When King Henry died, his son, Edward—Elizabeth's younger half-brother—was crowned king. But Edward soon died, and Mary—Elizabeth's older half-sister—became queen. Mary was hated by the people for marrying Prince Philip of Spain and executing anyone who didn't share her religious beliefs. Mary was so afraid that Elizabeth would plot against her that she had Elizabeth imprisoned in the Tower of London.

Elizabeth was eventually freed, but Mary remained suspicious and never trusted her.

When Mary died in 1558, Elizabeth became queen at age twenty-five. Elizabeth was a very different queen from her sister. She stopped the executions and refused to marry so that no man could take power away from her. Elizabeth had strong opinions about what was best for England, and she didn't hesitate to speak her mind. Most of all, she loved her people and her country. She often left the palace to visit the people. During a brutal war with Spain, she rode a horse to give a passionate speech to soldiers that inspired them to fight bravely.

Even though Elizabeth was beloved by the English people, she faced many plots and schemes. A distant cousin, Mary, Queen of Scots, tried to overthrow her. Years later, Elizabeth's dear friend, the Earl of Essex, plotted against her. She had them both executed for their betrayals.

Queen Elizabeth died on March 24, 1603, at age sixty-nine, but more than 400 years later, we still remember her as an example of powerful leadership.

Cesar Chavez was born on March 31, 1927, near Yuma, Arizona. When he wasn't attending the local school, Cesar helped his family work on his grandparents' ranch, which provided all they needed. Then everything changed. The Great Depression struck the United States, plunging millions of people into poverty. The Chavez family's ranch helped them survive those hard times, until a terrible drought spread across the land. The nearby canal dried up and the crops withered. The Chavezes had no choice but to move, or migrate, to California to look for work.

What Cesar experienced in California changed the course of his life. Wealthy farmers hired migrant workers and treated them terribly. The workers were paid very little—if they were paid at all. The Chavez family also endured racism against Mexican-Americans. Cesar saw how much the workers suffered and knew that something had to change.

When he grew up, Cesar started working for the Community Service Organization, which shared his belief that all people should be treated with decency and respect. He traveled from town to town, listening to the people's problems and helping them find solutions. His leadership abilities soon overcame his shyness. When Cesar talked, people listened. He had a gift for bringing people together, and he knew that change would only be possible if the people were united. To make that possible, he started a union called the National Farm Workers Association.

Cesar knew that violence was not the way he wanted to accomplish his goals. He encouraged people to use nonviolent tactics, including strikes, boycotts, and picket lines. He led a 300-mile march from the fields in Delano, California, to the state capitol in Sacramento, California. He even went on a hunger strike to bring attention to the cause. It took time, but all these methods combined put so much pressure on the farm owners that they agreed to better pay and conditions for the workers.

Cesar Chavez died on April 23, 1993. His birthday, March 31, is now known as Cesar Chavez Day. All over the United States, there are schools, parks, and other places named in his honor. Maybe there is one near you!

the TINY GENIUSES

THE TINY GENIUSES ARE LIVE, IN PERSON, AND READY TO HELP!

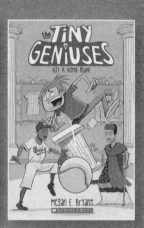

But can Jake Everdale keep his secret Heroes of History under wraps when the tiny toys are causing BIG problems?

SCHOLASTIC

scholastic.com

SCHOLASTIC and associated logos are trademarks and/or registered trademarks of Scholastic Inc.

TINYGENIUSES